Owlkids Books Inc.
10 Lower Spadina Avenue, Suite 400, Toronto, Ontario M5V 2Z2
www.owlkids.com

Published in France under the title *Mon imagier des petits bonheurs* © 2011
Éditions Escabelle, 11 rue Danielle Casanova, 92 500 Rueil Malmaison

Distributed in Canada by University of Toronto Press
5201 Dufferin Street, Toronto, Ontario M3H 5T8

Distributed in the United States by Publishers Group West
1700 Fourth Street, Berkeley, California 94710

Library and Archives Canada Cataloguing in Publication

Cordier, Séverine
     Picture my world / Séverine Cordier, Cynthia Lacroix.

Translation of: Mon imagier des petits bonheurs.
ISBN 978-1-926973-56-2

     1. Vocabulary--Juvenile literature. 2. Word recognition--
Juvenile literature. I. Lacroix, Cynthia II. Title.

PE1449.C675 2012   j428.1   C2011-908154-7

Library of Congress Control Number: 2011944602

Translator: Lesley Zimic

Canadian Patrimoine
Heritage canadien

Canada

Ontario
Ontario Media Development
Corporation

Canada Council   Conseil des Arts
for the Arts   du Canada

ONTARIO ARTS COUNCIL
CONSEIL DES ARTS DE L'ONTARIO

Société de développement
de l'industrie des médias
de l'Ontario

We acknowledge the financial support of the Canada Council for the Arts, the Ontario Arts Council,
the Government of Canada through the Canada Book Fund (CBF) and the Government of Ontario
through the Ontario Media Development Corporation's Book Initiative for our publishing activities.

Manufactured by Toppan Leefung Packaging & Printing (Dongguan) Co., Ltd.
Manufactured in Dongguan, China, in June 2012
Job #117094-2

A   B   C   D   E   F

Publisher of Chirp, chickaDEE and OWL
www.owlkids.com

PicTURE
mY WORLD

Séverine Cordier · Cynthia Lacroix

Book of the Month
July 2017
Julia

♡
love GG

"Look how you've grown!"

Holding hands

A new little sister

"Our new goldfish is named Arthur."

At the pool

"Don't bully my little sister."

"A bunny!"

"Cotton candy!"

"A car!"

"Just one!"

"Uh-oh,
Mommy forgot the keys."

"Tomorrow is the
first day of school."

"Not in my eyes."

A scraped knee

"When my little sister was born,
I got a new key chain!"

Feeling sick

"Let's pretend we're in a boat..."

"And what will
the young gentleman have?"

Splash!

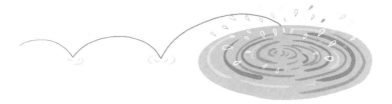

"It's MY doll!"

"Why are you pouting?"

"Hee-hee!"

"No!"

"Shh..."

"Where could it be?"

"Do you think it bites?"

"Tomorrow we'll make it even bigger."

"When I grow up,
I'm going to be a knight."

Ready to go

Picking cherries

"Why did it die?"

A scoop of strawberry
and a scoop of chocolate

"It rains, it pours."